P9-DED-197

The Littlest Uninvited One

By Charles Tazewell

Illustrated by Gail Tribble

Ideals Children's Books • Nashville, Tennessee
an imprint of Hambleton-Hill Publishing, Inc.

For my family, especially Grace.

—G.T.

Text copyright © 1998 by Linda Cheever
Illustrations copyright © 1998 Hambleton-Hill Publishing, Inc.

Published by Ideals Children's Books
An imprint of Hambleton-Hill Publishing, Inc.
1501 County Hospital Road
Nashville, Tennessee 37218
800-327-5113

Library of Congress Cataloging-in-Publication Data
Tazewell, Charles.
    The littlest uninvited one / by Charles Tazewell ; illustrated by Gail
Tribble. — 1st ed.
        p.   cm.
    Summary: A mischievous cherub named Michael brings a puppy to
Celestial City, causing an uproar that can be quieted only when the Son
orders that a place just for animals be constructed on the Street of Miracles.
    ISBN 1-57102-131-0 (hardcover)
    [1. Heaven—Fiction. 2. Dogs—Fiction. 3. Angels—Fiction] I. Tribble,
Gail, ill. II. Title.
    PZ7.T219Lv   1998
    [E]—dc21   98-16588
                                                                CIP
                                                                AC

The illustrations in this book were rendered in watercolor and colored
pencil.
The text type is set in Goudy.
The display type is set in Caslon Open and Goudy BoldItalic.

First Edition

10 9 8 7 6 5 4 3 2 1

One may sit in the great Plaza of Eternity for a thousand and one years as time is measured by human beings—but which is no more than a lazy summer afternoon in the Celestial City—listening to wondrous stories that delight and charm the ear.

Although it is situated in the old and original part of the city, many believe the Plaza to be the most beautiful spot in all Paradise. A full half of its magnificent perimeter is dominated by the massive Gates.

From its remaining half circle and extending fanwise to such farflung environs as the Elysian Fields, Fiddlers' Green and the Happy Hunting Grounds, sweep the broad avenues of Creation, Justice, Mercy, Compassion—and, of course, the most talked about, thought about, dreamed about street in all the universe—the winding Street of Miracles.

There is a story that is often told in the Plaza concerning the establishment at Number 10 on this Street of Miracles. The main building is of wood, a great oddity in the Celestial City, and is completely dwarfed by a series of huge annexes. The construction is crude and amateurish. It is a down-at-the-roof, crooked-at-the-beams, paint-bare building that should hang its head in shame as it stands there in the shadow of the majestic Hall of the Recording Angels and the imposing High Court of the Patriarch Prophets. On the contrary, there is a proud note in every creak of its ancient timbers; there is jovial laughter in every rumble of its old boards—for Number 10 knows that it is the most loved building in Paradise.

There might not be a Number 10 if it hadn't been for a cherub named Michael. This Michael bore not the slightest resemblance to all those well-behaved, dimpled cherubs who have flown so fluently from the brushes of the great masters. Indeed, many in his earthly neighborhood must have watched him and mentally voted him the most likely to become an imp.

His carroty hair was as cowlicked as a salt block in a pasture; to have counted the freckles on his snub-nosed face would have been as hopeless a task as tallying the stars in the Milky Way; his nervous fingers betrayed his rating of take-aparter first-class, who could quickly and permanently disassemble anything from a catapult to a mousetrap; each toe was a magnet for dust, sand and mud.

Since Michael had no relatives in the Celestial City, he was taken to the Angels' Aide, which was managed by a large corps of elderly grandmothers, well-remembered at some former earthly address for their overindulgence of their own grandchildren. Then, too, from its very beginning, this cherub shelter had always been under the direct supervision of one who loved and understood children—the only Son of the Proprietor of the Celestial City.

Michael liked his new home; he adored all the grandmothers; and he tolerated the other cherubs. It might be said, and truly said, that he was most agreeable and angelic—if we disregard the minor riot he caused when they tried to get him into a cherub's robe which had no pockets and which he declared was sissy. It took the grandmothers only four days to catch him—and when they showed Michael that the robe now had two large pockets sewed onto the back, he was almost seraphic about it in a grim sort of way.

At first, when Michael went strolling about the Celestial City—his wing tips thrust belligerently into the back pockets of his robe, his battered and limp halo hung on a red cowlick and a hasty prayer—he was the cause of much headshaking by the oldest archangels. They watched him turn cartwheels down the Avenue of Creation to impress a group of small girl-cherubs; they observed him sliding down the rail at the Museum of Antiquity and shouting "Whee-e-e!" instead of the more approved "Hallelujah!"; they saw him use his wings for a towel, whisk broom, handkerchief, pen-wiper and halo-shiner—and they sadly shook their beards and whispered that they didn't know what the younger generation of cherubs was coming to!

In time, however, since his coming seemed not to have shortened eternity by a single hour, Michael was accepted by everyone in the Celestial City as a genuine, albeit unconventional cherub.

Michael was a born explorer and, although the city covered a far greater area than time itself, his knowledge of its streets, avenues, boroughs and sub-divisions soon outmatched that of the earliest citizen and was second only to the Proprietor's. He could recite the names of all the long-lost ships that had found safe harbor with their crews at Fiddlers' Green; he knew the day and hour when the myriad campfires out at the Happy Hunting Grounds were kindled, forming clouds of aromatic smoke to bring the earth its Indian summer; he could walk blindfolded along any path through the Elysian Fields.

Michael's favorite place, however, was discovered quite by accident. Indeed, only a very few even knew of its existence, because it stood on a narrow and forgotten lane that ran alongside the great Wall in the oldest part of the city. It was named Eden Way and only a boy-cherub such as Michael would have been attracted to the square, cavernous building which stood at its end—and which bore the simple, utilitarian name, The Stables.

Time was—oh, so many long years ago—when The Stables had been filled with tumult and commotion. That was when the earth had been very new and its early settlers much perplexed because never before had they had a planet to manage. At all hours, huge chariots had rocketed out of The Stables, massive wheels rolling thunder and the hoofs of their fearsome steeds striking lightning, as they carried the Word of the Proprietor of the Celestial City down to the groundlings.

Now the earth was old. Now the great chariots stood idle and their fearsome steeds grew fat and lazy. Brawny Shard and his audacious crew of chariot drivers drowsed in the warmth of the eternal day; rousing now and then to snap at stones with whips which once had snapped at stars; wishing for a pair of new, receptive ears as bottomless at the Big Dipper into which to pour their stories of the good old days. Michael became their pet, their jewel and the cherub of their eye when they discovered that he had ears as fathomless as space and as absorbent as sponges.

Lying on the broad back of one of the awesome steeds while Shard polished a hoof, he would say, "Shard, do tell again how you carried the warning to Lot just before the Proprietor destroyed the wicked towns of Sodom and Gomorrah!" Or to boisterous Crag, who allowed Michael to ride with him in one of the rumbling chariots when he drove outside the great Gates to exercise a stamping team, "Crag—tell once more about the time that you drove the Proprietor, Himself, down to Mount Sinai to give Moses His Commandments!" And to jovial Shale, while Michael helped him at soaping and polishing the intricate harness, "Please, Shale, it's my favorite story! Tell about the night you drove the angel down to Judaea to tell the shepherds that the Proprietor's Son had been born in Bethlehem!"

One evening, when they were sitting in front of the Stables, the air sweetly perfumed by the night-blooming Cirrus clouds which clung ivylike to the great Wall, Michael heaved a small cherub sigh and asked, "Shard? Shard—what's your most favorite animal?"

"What size animal?" countered the practical Shard.

"Oh, about the size of a dog. With a tail like a dog. And ears like a dog."

"Well—if it looked that much like a dog, I'd call it a dog and I guess a dog would be my favorite," answered Shard.

"I wish," Michael said after a moment— "I wish I had a dog."

"Not allowed here," announced Crag.

"Who said so?" demanded Shale.

"Never has been one," said Crag. "And you know it."

"That doesn't signify!" cried Shale. "I leave it to Shard—all of us have been here right from the beginning—has the Proprietor ever said one word about no dogs?"

"No," Shard said judiciously, "not that I recollect."

"There you are, then!" bellowed Shale. "Now—the boy wants a dog. Why don't we get him a dog the next time we take a team out for exercise?"

"Who's arguing against it?" demanded Crag.

"Tomorrow's my day to drive," rumbled Shard.

"It's my day!" argued Shale.

"We'll all go!" decided Crag. "Any nitwit can select a robe, because it only needs to fit the outside of a boy. A dog, however, has to fit the outside and inside, and that requires mature thought and judgment!"

The dog of their choice would have been scorned by the average man or the average angel. It had a crook in its tail—but as Shard pointed out, the tail had such a friendly-frantic wag the defect would never be noticed. One ear stood up while the other ear hung down—but as Shale demonstrated, this really was a great blessing, because it gave the lucky animal not one, but two-dimensional hearing. Its coat was the tarnished brass of a sickly goldfish—but as Crag declared, it was a nice, compromising, neutral shade which was exactly right for the Celestial City, because it could never offend any race, creed or color. As for Michael, he was far richer in dog than Croesus ever had been in gold, and although occasionally he had been remiss about his evening prayers, he now meticulously thanked the Proprietor every night for having envisioned and created anything as marvelous as a dog!

After much thought and discussion, the pampered newcomer was christened Exodus, because, like the Israelites, he had journeyed out of one place into another. Once again The Stables was filled with tumult and commotion—and those passing the entrance to Eden Way often paused to listen to the booming guffaws of heavy voices, the joyous laughter of a child; or scratched puzzled heads with thoughtful wing tips at another sound which never before had been heard in the Celestial City—the shrill, cracked, voice-changing barking of Exodus.

As the planets revolved around a yellow sun, so did Michael's day revolve around a yellow dog. In the morning, there was the romp all over The Stables and up and down Eden Way; in the afternoon there were trips, with Exodus safely concealed under his robe, out to such far places as Valhalla, where cataracts of rainbows fell from towering cliffs to shatter on the rocks below and send their fragments streaming down to earth—or out to incredibly beautiful New Jerusalem, to which everyone in the Celestial City had contributed a tree, a flower, a brook or a winding lane from his dearest memory of childhood; in the evening there was the snuggling in the straw at The Stables with Exodus' heart thudding hard against his—and coming sweetly to the ear, the singing of Shard and the other drivers.

This ideal routine might have gone on forever if it hadn't been for the singing practice. Everyone had some part, large or small, and Michael, as a member of the cherub choir, was called for rehearsal.

He was on time for the first rehearsal by only the thickness of the slight tarnish on his halo, because it had taken him so long to say good-bye to Exodus, to admonish the drivers not to let him out of The Stables, and to give full instruction on what to do in case of any emergency such as a strain in his bark or a sprain in his tail. The cherub choir practice was not much of a success that day. In every song, Michael's voice was decidedly off-key and Michael's mind was definitely on—dog.

Their reunion that evening was jubilant. Shard, Shale and Crag, who had proved themselves to be consummate dog watchers, swaggered modestly under Michael's praise, while Exodus employed a pink tongue to wash each freckle, erasing every foreign odor it had gathered during the day so that Michael would again smell like The Stables.

The next morning, reassured by the outcome of the day before, Michael dashed out of Angels' Aide, darted down Eden Way to say good-bye to Exodus, and then raced off to singing practice—arriving with a full split second to spare. Of all cherub faces, his was the shiniest. Of all cherub voices, his was the lustiest. Of all cherub scents, his was the doggiest.

The person or object responsible for the first link in a chain of unhappy events which later led to catastrophe has never been irrefutably ascertained. Shale put the blame on a defective latch. Crag put the blame on a defective staple. Shard put the blame on both their defective heads. Whatever failed or whoever was at fault, the gate of The Stable stood three inches ajar and Exodus wiggled out.

Reading Michael's footsteps up Eden Way was an easy task for Exodus' young, primary-grade nose, but when he arrived at the Plaza of Eternity, where every day thousands upon thousands passed, he lost the trail. He hopefully examined the steps of the Library of the Archangels; he anxiously sniffed the doorstep of the High Court of the Patriarch Prophets; he frantically inspected every inch of the curb in front of the House of the Guardian and Trustful Angels; his fear turned into dread and his dread into terror as he minutely nosed the entrance of the Museum of Antiquity and found no trace of Michael's feet.

At this moment, a passer-by noticed him and bent down to pat him, and Exodus, legs trembling and suddenly remembering unkind hands of earlier days, shied away and gave a shrill bark of alarm! This sound, never before heard in the Plaza of Eternity, caused every head to turn—and then, because the people who lived in the Celestial City were much like the people who lived in any city, everyone hurried across the Plaza to assume the role of curious bystander.

Exodus, finding himself surrounded by this host of strangers, cowered and whimpered. Then, with courage born of panic, he snarled a vicious string of mongrel growls, threw himself at the forest of legs, slithered through to freedom and went bolting down the Avenue of Creation! It was blind, unreasoning flight. The voices behind him and those along his way which called to him only added to his fear and he went faster and faster until he was a yellow comet with a yellow tail flying through the Celestial City.

He made a shambles of Halosmith Road—scattering the workers like chaff—toppling the towering piles of golden circlets which went rolling and bouncing off into infinity! Centuries hence they would confound the earthlings, who, with bated breath, would tell their awe-struck tales of saucers flying past.

He left chaos behind him in the bazaars of Robemakers Lane. Just before his arrival, a whisper as fast and as darting as a hummingbird had sped down the street—a hound of hades, breathing fire and brimstone, was loose—in the Celestial City!

Upon the appearance of this satanic emissary, every seamstress swooned or had hysterics, and league upon league of finest weaving of every rainbow hue went streaming off into space! A thousand years from then, when it had been woven into tapestries by the four winds, the groundlings would ask their men of science to explain the season's sunsets of unearthly beauty.

Exodus was outmaneuvered and brought to bay in the Street of the Wingmakers by a company of Avenging Angels, the most feared and implacable soldiers of all time. In an instant, they could destroy a city; in a week, they could starve a nation with hordes of locusts or other insects; in a month, they could decimate a continent with a plague; in forty days and forty nights, they could drown a planet. Strange to say, these dread avengers were very gentle with Exodus. The ferocious sergeant surprised the onlookers by talking puppy-talk—and the merciless captain, looking neither to right nor left, strode off to the High Court of the Patriarch Prophets with Exodus cradled in his arms.

It was the unanimous decision of the Patriarch Prophets that Exodus was to be banished from the Celestial City at the first hour of the following day, which was the Hour of Correlation when every planet, star, sun and meteor was checked for path and position against the Proprietor's Master Plan of Creation. Until that time, he was to be confined in the old Gatehouse, an abandoned relic of the early days when there had been few arrivals.

The Patriarch Prophets, serene in their belief that the matter of the yellow dog was settled, went on to more important business; but being mere prophets and not the Proprietor, they could not be all-knowing. The next morning, at the Hour of Correlation, the planets, suns, stars and comets were all in their proper places, but there was no Exodus in the old Gatehouse and there was a red-haired cherub missing at Angels' Aide.

The Celestial City was searched street by street and avenue by avenue. Each distant borough was thoroughly combed and every possibly hiding place—even though it was as small as a needle's eye—was looked into, but not a red or yellow hair could be found. The elderly grandmothers at Angels' Aide, all of a flutter because never before had they lost a cherub, made their heart-stricken, incoherent report to the Only Son of the Proprietor of the Celestial City.

The Son listened and smiled and nodded His head. Then, unlike all the others, because He has always been very knowing about children, He searched nowhere in the Celestial City for Michael and the yellow dog. When He left Angels' Aide, He turned and made His way across the Plaza of Eternity, passed through the great Gates and walked slowly down the Stairs. On the bottommost step, scarcely visible in the cold, whirling mists and empty darkness of endless space, He saw a red blob and a yellow blob which appeared to be tightly fused together.

The Proprietor's Son sat down on the step and said: "Would you mind if I petted your dog? I've been standing there admiring him—and do you know that in all my travels, I don't believe I've ever seen such a handsome animal."

"They don't like him—and they don't think he's at all handsome!" The cherub's words were so hushed and tear-soaked that no one but the Only Son of the Proprietor could have heard and understood them. "They're going to send him away!"

"Oh, that's a great mistake," said the Son.

"I won't stay if he has to go!" wept Michael.

"I don't blame you for feeling that way—because I can see that you and this dog are the best of friends." The Son gently stroked the rough yellow fur. "I once had one that was very much like him. Oh, not nearly so fine, of course—but I thought he was beautiful. We met quite by accident. He was a stray that had sought shelter under the same roof where I was born—and when we left that place and went into Egypt, he followed right along at our little donkey's heels."

"What was his name?"

"I called him Caleb. Oh, he was very smart. And when I was a boy in Nazareth, he went everywhere with me and guarded my bed every night." The Son smiled at the memory of long ago. "Now you must tell me how you came by your friend."

The Son listened to Michael's story, gravely nodding His head from time to time. Then, when it was finished, He rose and held out His hand.

"Come, Michael," He said. "Let us go back into the City."

"But if I go back, they'll take Exodus away from me!" cried the cherub.

"Oh, no," said the Son. "Has it not been promised by the Proprietor that all men shall find what they love and cherish in His Celestial City? And how very blind We have been never to have seen that men would give such a great share of their love to all the small creatures that live with them their days on earth. Ah, what an empty, lonely place Our Celestial City must be for those who believe that the familiar and never forgotten voice of a furred or feathered friend is more sweet and more harmonious than the sound of all Our angel choirs. Come!" He lifted the cherub to his feet. "Come, Michael, we must do something about it, you and I!"

Carrying the cherub in His arms and with a small yellow dog following closely at His heels, the Son of the Proprietor walked up the broad, foot-worn Stairs and passed through the great Gates.

At all hours, in the busy days that followed, the huge chariots rocketed as of old up and down Eden Way—massive wheels rolling thunder and the flying hoofs of the fearsome steeds striking lightning as they did the bidding of the Proprietor and His Only Son! The frightened earthlings ran into their houses and covered their heads as the sky was slashed into fiery ribbons and trampled into ominous clouds of black dust, and they trembled as the ground beneath their feet quavered and shook and groaned under the mighty laboring of all the Heavenly Host!

When the task was finished, when the last great timber and smallest peg had been found and carried to the Celestial City, there arose on the Street of Miracles, in the shadow of the majestic Hall of the Recording Angels and the imposing High Court of the Patriarch Prophets, the shabby, down-at-the-roof, crooked-at-the-beams building which stands there today with its many additions.

The old walls are impregnated with the smell and the warmth of many animals, for here is safely sheltered every small creature that anyone has ever loved and lost. No owner need ever worry about their care or comfort, for in this wondrous place are a man and a woman who were summoned by the Proprietor from their retirement at Elysian Fields and who joyfully resumed the work they knew so well.

Whenever the door at Number 10 opens and a new visitor appears, there is instantly an excited chorus of barks, meows, chirps, squeaks and chattering. Suddenly, from somewhere—perhaps the farthest corner—there comes a sharp. ecstatic and almost hysterical cry which rises high above all the others. The ear and the heart then know that the long lost is lost no longer.

Number 10 is very easy to find. In the Plaza of Eternity will be found a red-haired cherub and a yellow dog. Following the robe with the pockets in the back and wagging tail with a crook in it, the newcomer will arrive in no time at all at the famous Ark of Captain and Mrs. Noah at Number 10 on the Street of Miracles.